Classic Tales

Level 1

The Little Red Hen

Retold by Sue Arengo
Illustrated by Bruno Robert

Contents

The Little Red Hen	2
Exercises	20
Picture Dictionary	22
About *Classic Tales*	24

OXFORD
UNIVERSITY PRESS

 Here is the little red hen.
And here are her friends –
Cat, Duck, and Goose.

2

'Look!' says the little red hen. 'Seeds!
Wheat seeds! Let's plant them!
Come on! Who can help me?'

'Come on! Who can help me?'
says the little red hen.

'I can't,' says Cat. 'I want to sleep.'

Who can help me?

I can't.

'Who can help me?'
says the little red hen.

'I can't,' says Duck. 'I want
to play in the water.'

'Come on!' says the little red hen. 'Who can help me?'

'I can't,' says Goose. 'I want to sit in the sun.'

All right.

'All right,' says the little red hen. And she does all the work. She plants all the seeds.

'The seeds want water. Who can help me?' says the little red hen.

The seeds want water.

'Who can help me?'

'I can't,' says Cat. 'I don't like water.'

'Come on!' says the little red hen. 'Who can help me?'

'I can't,' says Duck. 'I want my lunch.'

Who can help me?

I can't.

'Who can help me?'

'I can't,' says Goose. 'I want a walk.'

'All right,' says the little red hen.
And she does all the work.

All right.

The sun is warm. The wheat grows.
It grows big and green.

The sun is hot. And now
the wheat is yellow.

We can cut it now.

'Look!' says the little red hen.
'The wheat is yellow. We can cut
it now. Who can help me?'

'Who can help me?'
'I can't,' says Cat. 'I want to play.'

I can't.

Who can help me?

'Who can help me?'
'I can't,' says Duck.
'I want my lunch.'

'Who can help me?'
'I can't,' says Goose. 'I want to play.'

'All right,' says the little red hen.
And she does all the work. She cuts
all the wheat.

'Let's grind this wheat,'
says the little red hen.
'Let's grind it into flour.
Who can help me?'

'I can't,' says Cat.
'I want some milk.'

Who can help me?

12

'Who can help me?'
'I can't,' says Duck.
'I want to sleep.'

'Who can help me?'
'I can't,' says Goose.
'I want a drink.'

I want to sleep.

'All right,' says the little red hen. And she does all the work. She grinds the wheat into flour.

'We can make bread,' says the little red hen. 'We can make some bread with this flour.'

'Come on!' says the little red hen. 'Who can help me?'

'I can't,' says Cat. 'I want to sleep.'

'Come on!' says the little red hen. 'Who can help me?'

'I can't,' says Duck. 'I want to go in the garden.'

I want to *go* in the *garden*.

'Who can help me?'
says the little red hen.

'I can't,' says Goose.
'I want to sit and wash.'

I want to sit and wash.

'All right,' says the little red hen.
And she does all the work. She
makes all the bread.

'This bread looks good!' says the little red hen. 'It's time to eat the bread. Who can help me?'

It's time to eat the bread.

'I can!' says Cat.

'I can!' says Duck.

'I can!' says Goose.

But the little red hen thinks.
'No!' she says. 'You can't!
Off you go! Go away and play!'

And she eats all the bread.
All … all … all the bread.

1 What do they say? Write the words.

1

2

3

I want to s_leep_ .

I want to p_____ in the water.

I want to s_____ and w_____ .

2 Who wants what? Join the words and write sentences.

1 Goose

2 Duck

3 The seeds

4 Cat

5 Goose, Cat, and Duck

6 Hen

want

wants

some milk.

some water.

some help.

a drink.

some lunch.

some bread.

1 _Goose wants a drink._

2 _____

3 _____

4 _____

5 _____

6 _____

3 How does the little red hen make bread?
Number the sentences 1–8.

- ☐ The wheat is yellow.
- ☐ 1 The hen has some wheat seeds.
- ☐ The hen grinds the wheat into flour.
- ☐ The wheat grows.
- ☐ The hen makes bread with the flour.
- ☐ The hen cuts the wheat.
- ☐ The seeds have water.
- ☐ The hen plants the seeds.

4 Write the end of the story again, correcting
the mistake in each sentence.

Cat, Duck, and Goose help the little red hen make the bread. The bread doesn't look good. The little red hen doesn't eat all the bread. She wants Cat, Duck, and Goose to help her. Cat, Duck, and Goose have bread for their lunch.

Cat, Duck, and Goose don't help the little red hen make the
bread.

_____

_____

_____

_____

_____

Picture Dictionary

bread

friends

cut

garden

drink

go away

duck

goose

flour

grind

grow

sleep

hen

think

lunch

warm *It's warm.*

milk

wash

plant

water

seeds

wheat

23

Classic Tales

Classic stories retold for learners of English – bringing the magic of traditional storytelling to the language classroom

Level 1: 100 headwords
- The Enormous Turnip
- The Little Red Hen
- Lownu Mends the Sky
- The Magic Cooking Pot
- Mansour and the Donkey
- Peach Boy
- The Princess and the Pea
- Rumplestiltskin
- The Shoemaker and the Elves
- Three Billy-Goats

Level 2: 150 headwords
- Amrita and the Trees
- Big Baby Finn
- The Fisherman and his Wife
- The Gingerbread Man
- Jack and the Beanstalk
- Thumbelina
- The Town Mouse and the Country Mouse
- The Ugly Duckling

Level 3: 200 headwords
- Aladdin
- Goldilocks and the Three Bears
- The Little Mermaid
- Little Red Riding Hood

Level 4: 300 headwords
- Cinderella
- The Goose Girl
- Sleeping Beauty
- The Twelve Dancing Princesses

Level 5: 400 headwords
- Beauty and the Beast
- The Magic Brocade
- Pinocchio
- Snow White and the Seven Dwarfs

All *Classic Tales* have an accompanying
- **e-Book with Audio Pack** containing the book and the e-book with audio, for use on a computer or CD player. Teachers can also project the e-book onto an interactive whiteboard to use it like a Big Book.
- **Activity Book and Play** providing extra language practice and the story adapted as a play for performance in class or on stage.

For more details, visit
www.oup.com/elt/readers/classictales

OXFORD
UNIVERSITY PRESS

Great Clarendon Street, Oxford OX2 6DP

Oxford University Press is a department of the University of Oxford. It furthers the University's objective of excellence in research, scholarship, and education by publishing worldwide in

Oxford New York

Auckland Cape Town Dar es Salaam Hong Kong Karachi
Kuala Lumpur Madrid Melbourne Mexico City Nairobi
New Delhi Shanghai Taipei Toronto

With offices in

Argentina Austria Brazil Chile Czech Republic France Greece
Guatemala Hungary Italy Japan Poland Portugal Singapore
South Korea Switzerland Thailand Turkey Ukraine Vietnam

OXFORD and OXFORD ENGLISH are registered trade marks of Oxford University Press in the UK and in certain other countries

This edition © Oxford University Press 2011

The moral rights of the author have been asserted

Database right Oxford University Press (maker)

First published in Classic Tales 2004

2015 2014 2013 2012 2011

10 9 8 7 6 5 4 3 2 1

ISBN: 978 0 19 423870 0

This *Classic Tale* title is available as an e-Book with Audio Pack
ISBN: 978 0 19 423873 1

Also available: *The Little Red Hen* Activity Book and Play
ISBN: 978 0 19 423871 7

Printed in China

This book is printed on paper from certified and well-managed sources.

ACKNOWLEDGEMENTS

Illustrated by: Bruno Robert / Plum Pudding Illustration

prince

stone

princess

storm

queen

tea

quilt

visit

ride

wet *It is wet.*

sit up

wind

Classic Tales

Classic stories retold for learners of English – bringing the magic of traditional storytelling to the language classroom

Level 1: 100 headwords
- The Enormous Turnip
- The Little Red Hen
- Lownu Mends the Sky
- The Magic Cooking Pot
- Mansour and the Donkey
- Peach Boy
- The Princess and the Pea
- Rumpelstiltskin
- The Shoemaker and the Elves
- Three Billy-Goats

Level 2: 150 headwords
- Amrita and the Trees
- Big Baby Finn
- The Fisherman and his Wife
- The Gingerbread Man
- Jack and the Beanstalk
- Thumbelina
- The Town Mouse and the Country Mouse
- The Ugly Duckling

Level 3: 200 headwords
- Aladdin
- Goldilocks and the Three Bears
- The Little Mermaid
- Little Red Riding Hood

Level 4: 300 headwords
- Cinderella
- The Goose Girl
- Sleeping Beauty
- The Twelve Dancing Princesses

Level 5: 400 headwords
- Beauty and the Beast
- The Magic Brocade
- Pinocchio
- Snow White and the Seven Dwarfs

All *Classic Tales* have an accompanying
- **e-Book with Audio Pack** containing the book and the e-book with audio, for use on a computer or CD player. Teachers can also project the e-book onto an interactive whiteboard to use it like a Big Book.
- **Activity Book and Play** providing extra language practice and the story adapted as a play for performance in class or on stage.

For more details, visit
www.oup.com/elt/readers/classictales

OXFORD
UNIVERSITY PRESS

Great Clarendon Street, Oxford, OX2 6DP, United Kingdom

Oxford University Press is a department of the University of Oxford. It furthers the University's objective of excellence in research, scholarship, and education by publishing worldwide. Oxford is a registered trade mark of Oxford University Press in the UK and in certain other countries

© Oxford University Press 2011

The moral rights of the author have been asserted

First published in Classic Tales 2004

2015 2014 2013 2012 2011

10 9 8 7 6 5 4 3 2 1

ISBN: 978 0 19 423878 6

This *Classic Tale* title is available as an e-Book with Audio Pack
ISBN: 978 0 19 423881 6

Also available: *The Princess and the Pea Activity Book and Play*
ISBN: 978 0 19 423879 3

Printed in China

This book is printed on paper from certified and well-managed sources.

ACKNOWLEDGEMENTS

Illustrated by: Michelle Lamoreaux/Shannon Associates